PZ
7
F26
A4

PZ7.F26A4

A041107301

P9-CDU-969

SENECA
SHEPPARD
COLLEGE LIBRARY

SENECA
NEWNHAM
COLLEGE LIBRARY

Date Due

Feb21'73		
MAY 2 3 1978	APR 2 9	
NOV 6 1978	JUN 7 1990	
Apr. 1	FEB 1 1 1991	
NOV 1 8 1981		
	APR 1 1 1991	
MAR 9 1982	APR 2 5 1991	
	OCT 0 8 1992	
MAY 5 1988	NOV 0 2 1993	
MAY 9 1986	DEC 1 3 1994	
May 16/86		
MAR 1 1 1987		

SENECA
SHEPPARD
COLLEGE LIBRARY

SENECA
NEWNHAM
COLLEGE LIBRARY

SENECA
FINCH
COLLEGE LIBRARY

ALL ALONE
WITH DADDY

ALL ALONE
WITH DADDY

by Joan Fassler

illustrated by Dorothy Lake Gregory

Behavioral Publications, Inc.
New York

CHILDREN'S SERIES ON PSYCHOLOGICALLY RELEVANT THEMES

Titles

DON'T WORRY, DEAR	ALL ALONE WITH DADDY	I HAVE FEELINGS
THE MAN OF THE HOUSE	MY GRANDPA DIED TODAY	BILLY AND OUR NEW BABY
ONE LITTLE GIRL	THE BOY WITH A PROBLEM	THINGS I HATE

Review Committee:

Leonard S. Blackman, Ph.D.
Teachers College, Columbia University

Gerald Caplan, M.D.
Harvard Medical School

Eli M. Bower, Ed.D.
National Institute of
Mental Health

Series Editor:
Sheldon R. Roen, Ph.D.

Copyright© 1969 by Behavioral Publications, Inc.
2852 Broadway—Morningside Heights
New York, N.Y. 10025

Illustrations copyright© 1969 by M. Jane Smyth

All rights reserved. Except for use in a review, the reproduction or utilization of this work in any form or by any electronic, mechanical, or other means, now known or hereafter invented, including photocopying and recording, and in any information storage and retrieval system is forbidden without the written permission of the publisher.

Production by Bob Vari

Manufactured in the United States of America

Library of Congress Catalog Card Number 76-80120

For my own little girl,
Ellen Fassler

Ellen was a little girl with yellow hair. She was four years old. One evening Ellen's mother packed a small suitcase and went away on a trip to visit Ellen's grandma. And Ellen and her daddy stayed behind at home.

On the very first morning that her mother was away, Ellen got up early. Then she tiptoed to her mother's dresser and she tried on some of her mother's lipstick. And her powder. And even some eyebrow pencil. Then she put on a necklace, and earrings, and sunglasses, and high-heeled shoes. And perfume, too.

When she was all finished, her daddy woke up. "I'm grown-up now, daddy, and I want to marry you," Ellen said. Ellen's daddy laughed at her. "You can't marry me," he said, as he helped her wash the makeup off her face. But he told her she was very, very pretty and she didn't even need any makeup at all. And that made Ellen feel very good inside.

Then Ellen's daddy said that she could go downstairs and set the breakfast table. And Ellen did. She put a spoon, and a fork, and a knife at daddy's place. Then she poured a great big glass of orange juice for him. And she wiped up all the little spills and splashes very carefully. Then she sat herself down in the mommy chair.

"Can I make pancakes for you?" Ellen asked her daddy when he came to the table.

"No," laughed Ellen's daddy, "you can't make pancakes for me." But he drank every drop of the juice and he hugged and kissed her, too. And that made Ellen feel very good inside.

Later that day Ellen and her daddy
took a walk in the park. And Ellen felt
especially good because she especially
loved being all alone with daddy.

That night, when Ellen's daddy was getting ready for bed, he found a funny little bump under the blanket in the big mommy and daddy bed.

"No," said daddy, when the bump moved. "You can't sleep where mommy sleeps." But he smiled at Ellen and he put his arm around her. And he let her stay just a little while. And that made Ellen feel very good inside, too.

The next day Ellen's mother came home.

Now Ellen's mother wore the makeup and the jewelry and the high heels. And Ellen's daddy told Ellen's mother that she was very pretty.

Now Ellen's mother sat in the mommy chair at the breakfast table. And Ellen's mother poured the orange juice. And she made two batches of pancakes. Ellen's daddy said that they were delicious. And he ate them all up.

Now, when Ellen and daddy went for a walk in the park, mommy came along, too. Ellen was glad that mommy came along. But she remembered how especially good it felt to be all alone with daddy. And now she wasn't all alone with daddy any more at all.

Now Ellen's mother slept in the big bed with Ellen's daddy. And there was no more room in the mommy and daddy bed for a little girl. Even a little girl who only made a very small bump in the blanket. So Ellen didn't feel quite so good inside any more at all.

When Ellen went to sleep that night, she dreamed about brides and weddings and pretty, lacy veils. And little girls who grew up and really did marry their daddys. And had little boy babies for them, too.

When she woke up, Ellen thought about her dream. And deep, deep down inside herself Ellen really did wish that she could marry her daddy some day. But, of course, she knew she never could.

But she COULD grow up to be very much
like her mother.

And she COULD grow up to marry some-
one very much like her daddy.

And that is just exactly what Ellen did.

SENECA
SHEPPARD
COLLEGE LIBRARY

SENECA
FINCH
COLLEGE LIBRARY